Here's what kids have to say about reading Magic Tree House® books and Magic Tree House® Merlin Missions:

Thank you for writing these great books! I have learned a great deal of information about history and the world around me.—Rosanna

Your series, the Magic Tree House, was really influential on my late childhood years. [Jack and Annie] taught me courage through their rigorous adventures and profound friendship, and how they stuck it out through thick and thin, from start to finish.—Joe

Your description is fantastic! The words pop out... oh, man... [the Magic Tree House series] is really exciting!—Christina

I like the Magic Tree House series. I stay up all night reading them. Even on school nights!—Peter

I think I've read about twenty-five of your Magic Tree House books! I'm reading every Magic Tree House book I can get my hands on!—Jack

Never stop writing, and if you can't think about anything to write about, don't worry, use some of my ideas!!—Kevin

Parents, teachers, and librarians love Magic Tree House® books, too!

[Magic Tree House] comes up quite a bit at parent/ teacher conferences. . . . The parents are amazed at how much more reading is being done at home because of your books. I am very pleased to know such fun and interesting reading exists for students. . . . Your books have also made students want to learn more about the places Jack and Annie visit. What wonderful starters for some research projects!—Kris L.

As a librarian, I have seen many happy young readers coming into the library to check out the next Magic Tree House book in the series. I have assisted young library patrons with finding nonfiction materials related to the Magic Tree House book they have read. . . . The message you are sending to children is invaluable: siblings can be friends; boys and girls can hang out together. . . .—Lynne H.

[My daughter] had a slow start reading, but somehow with your Magic Tree House series, she has been inspired and motivated to read. It is with such urgency that she tracks down your books. She often blurts out various facts and lines followed by "I read that in my Magic Tree House book."—Jenny E.

[My students] seize every opportunity they can to reread a Magic Tree House book or look at all the wonderful illustrations. Jack and Annie have opened a door to a world of literacy that I know will continue throughout the lives of my students.—Deborah H.

[My son] carries his Magic Tree House books everywhere he goes. He just can't put the book he is reading down until he finishes it. . . . He is doing better in school overall since he has made reading a daily thing. He even has a bet going with his aunt that if he continues doing well in school, she will continue to buy him the next book in the Magic Tree House series.—Rosalie R.

MAGIC TREE HOUSE® #39
A MERLIN MISSION

Dark Day in the Deep Sea

by Mary Pope Osborne

illustrated by Sal Murdocca

SCHOLASTIC INC.

New York Toronto London Auckland
Sydney Mexico City New Delhi Hong Kong

ISBN-13: 978-0-545-20214-5
ISBN-10: 0-545-20214-0

Text copyright © 2008 by Mary Pope Osborne.
Illustrations copyright © 2008 by Sal Murdocca. All rights reserved.
Published by Scholastic Inc., 557 Broadway, New York, NY 10012, by arrangement with Random House Children's Books, a division of Random House, Inc. Magic Tree House is a registered trademark of Mary Pope Osborne; used under license. SCHOLASTIC and associated logos are trademarks and/or registered trademarks of Scholastic Inc.

12 11 10 9 8 7 6 5 4 3 2 1   9 10 11 12 13 14/0

Printed in the U.S.A.   40

First Scholastic printing, September 2009

For Elyot and Beatrice Harmston

Dear Reader,

For three years of my childhood, my family lived right on the ocean. Our windows were always covered with sea spray from the waves splashing on the rocks beneath the house. You might think I spent every summer playing in the water. But sadly, I was afraid of the ocean. I was convinced that sea creatures would grab me, sting me, swish against me, bite me, or drown me. (Sometimes having too much imagination can be a problem!)

I did try very hard to overcome my fear. Many times I waded in cautiously—wearing my sneakers!—one step at a time. I wish I could tell you that one day I got up the courage and just dove in and was never afraid again. But alas, I never managed to get in past my knees.

Only as a grown-up did I realize that the creatures of the sea were probably more afraid of me than I was of them. Since learning this, I have not been afraid—in fact, I've gone snorkeling in the waters of the Caribbean and have swum with dolphins off the coast of Mexico. My fear of ocean life has been replaced with great wonder and respect. I hope by the time you finish this book, you'll feel the same.

Mary Pope Osborne

CONTENTS

"The sea, once it casts its spell, holds one in its net of wonder forever."

—Jacques Cousteau

Prologue

One summer day in Frog Creek, Pennsylvania, a mysterious tree house appeared in the woods. A brother and sister named Jack and Annie soon learned that the tree house was magic—it could take them to any time and any place in history. They also learned that the tree house belonged to Morgan le Fay, a magical librarian from the legendary realm of Camelot.

After Jack and Annie traveled on many adventures for Morgan, Merlin the magician began sending them on "Merlin Missions" in the tree house. With help from two young sorcerers named Teddy and Kathleen, Jack and Annie visited four *mythical* places and found valuable objects to help save Camelot.

On their next four Merlin Missions, Jack and Annie once again traveled to real times and real places in history: Venice, Baghdad, Paris, and New York City. After proving to Merlin that they knew how to use magic wisely, he awarded them the Wand of Dianthus, a powerful magic wand that would help them make their own magic.

On their last two adventures, Teddy and Kathleen told Jack and Annie that Merlin was very unhappy and not well and that Morgan wanted them to search for four secrets of happiness to share with Merlin.

Now Jack and Annie are waiting for the tree house to return and take them on their third mission to help Merlin. . . .

CHAPTER ONE

Back to the Sea

Jack felt raindrops. He looked up and saw a summer storm cloud.

"Hurry!" Jack called to Annie. They were riding their bikes home from the library. Jack's backpack was filled with library books. He didn't want them to get wet.

As Jack and Annie pedaled faster, a large white bird swooped over them and flew into the Frog Creek woods.

"Did you see that?" cried Jack.

"A seagull!" called Annie. "It's a sign!"

"You're right!" said Jack. The last time they'd seen a seagull in Frog Creek, the magic tree house was waiting for them!

"The woods!" said Annie.

Jack and Annie bumped their bikes over the curb. The rain fell harder as they headed into the wet woods. Their bike tires bounced over the rough ground, crushing leaves and snapping twigs.

"It must be time to look for another secret of happiness for Merlin!" Jack called.

"I hope Merlin's feeling better!" shouted Annie.

"I hope Teddy and Kathleen came with the tree house!" shouted Jack.

"Me too!" shouted Annie.

Jack and Annie steered their bikes under canopies of wet leaves. By the time they came to the tallest oak in the woods, the seagull had disappeared. But the magic tree house was back! It was high in the tallest oak, its rope ladder swaying in the wind and rain.

Jack and Annie climbed off their bikes and propped them against the trunk of the tree.

"Teddy! Kathleen!" Annie shouted.

There was no answer.

"I guess they didn't come this time," Jack said.

"Darn!" said Annie. "I really wanted to see them."

"Boo!" Two older kids looked down out of the tree house window: a curly-haired boy with a big grin and a girl with sea-blue eyes and a beautiful smile. Both were wearing long green cloaks.

"Yay!" cried Annie and Jack.

The rain fell harder as they started up the rope ladder. When they climbed into the tree house, they yanked off their bike helmets and hugged Teddy and Kathleen.

"Morgan sent us to tell you about your next mission for Merlin," said Teddy.

"How *is* Merlin?" asked Annie.

Teddy stopped smiling. He shook his head.

"Merlin still suffers from an unspoken sorrow," Kathleen said sadly.

"When can we see him?" asked Annie.

"We've learned two secrets of happiness to share with him," said Jack.

"You may visit him after you have learned two more secrets," said Kathleen. "Morgan believes four is the magic number that will ensure success."

"We have come to send you on your search for a third secret," said Teddy.

Kathleen took a book from under her cloak and handed it to Jack and Annie. "From Morgan's hands to our hands to yours," she said.

Jack took the book from her. The cover showed waves crashing on a beach.

"Wow," said Jack. "We're going to the ocean?"

"Yes," said Teddy. "That is where you will next search for a secret of happiness."

"The ocean always makes me happy," said Annie. "Once Jack and I traveled to a coral reef and swam with dolphins. And we ran into an octopus. But he was nice and shy and—"

"But the shark we saw *wasn't* shy," Jack broke in. "It was a big hammerhead."

"Oh, my," said Kathleen.

"We took a ride in a mini-sub," said Annie. "It was so cool!"

"Until it started to leak and—" said Jack.

"We had to escape!" said Annie.

"Yeah," said Jack. "We tried not to splash—so the shark wouldn't notice us."

"We had so much fun!" said Annie.

Kathleen smiled. "Well, I hope you will not find the same 'fun' on this journey," she said.

"But in case you do, you have your wand to help you, do you not?" asked Teddy. "The Wand of Dianthus?"

"Of course," said Jack. "I always carry it, just in case." Jack reached into his backpack and pulled out the silvery wand. It was shaped like the spiraled horn of a unicorn.

"You remember the three rules?" asked Kathleen.

"Sure," said Jack. "To make magic, we use a wish with only five words."

"And before we use the wand, we have to try our hardest," said Annie.

"And the wand can only be used for the good of others," said Jack, "not just ourselves."

"Exactly," said Teddy.

"I wonder who the 'others' will be on this mission," said Annie. She looked at Teddy and Kathleen. "Maybe you guys?"

"I fear not," said Kathleen. "You must find the third secret on your own."

"Just remember to keep your wits about you," said Teddy.

"And listen to your hearts," said Kathleen.

"Okay," said Annie. "We'll tell you all about it when we see you again."

Lightning flashed through the woods as Jack pointed to the cover of the ocean book. "I wish we could go there!" he said.

Thunder cracked in the dark sky. The wind blew harder.

The tree house started to spin.

It spun faster and faster.

Then everything was still.

Absolutely still.

CHAPTER TWO

Pirates Again?

Jack opened his eyes. Teddy and Kathleen were gone. The warm air was filled with mist.

Jack and Annie peered out the window together. The tree house had landed in a tall tree with spreading branches. The mist was so thick they couldn't see anything around them. But Jack heard the caws of gulls and the swooshing of rolling waves. He smelled salt water and sea-weed.

"The ocean's out there. Feel it?" said Annie.

"I hear it and smell it," said Jack.

"Then let's go play in it!" said Annie. She pulled off her sneakers and socks.

"We can't just *play*," Jack said. "We have to look for a secret of happiness."

"Well, I'm happiest when I'm playing in the ocean!" Annie started down the rope ladder.

I'm sure our mission's harder than that, Jack thought. He took their library books out of his pack and replaced them with the deep-sea book.

"Hurry!" said Annie.

Jack put on his pack and started down after her. He stepped off the ladder onto the misty ground.

"Come on!" said Annie.

Jack followed Annie toward the sounds of seabirds and waves. They walked through feathery ferns and climbed a sloping sand dune. When they rounded the top, Jack saw waves rolling onto a wide, sandy beach. But the ocean itself was still shrouded in a gray haze.

"Wow," said Annie.

"Yeah," said Jack.

"Come on, let's go in," Annie said.

Jack and Annie hurried down the dune and ran toward the ocean. While Annie waded into the water, Jack stood at the edge and pulled out their research book. "Listen to this, Annie," he called.

Jack read loudly:

> **Water covers three-quarters of our earth. Most of the ocean is an enormous plain a little more than two miles deep. But some ocean trenches are more than six miles deep.**

"More than six miles?" Annie asked, splashing the water with her hands. "It's six miles from our house to Aunt Libby's."

"I know," said Jack. He read more:

> **The ocean is home to thousands and thousands of sea creatures. Mountains and volcanoes are also hidden deep beneath the surface of the sea.**

"Mountains and volcanoes?" asked Annie. "Under the water?"

"That's what the book says," said Jack. "The ocean's a whole world we don't know anything about."

"Well, *some* people know about it," said Annie. "Or that book couldn't have been written."

Good point, thought Jack.

"Put the book away and come in, Jack," said Annie. "The sun's coming out!"

Jack looked up from his book. The sun was burning away the mist, making the day hotter.

"Let's go swimming!" said Annie.

As Annie dove into a wave, Jack put his book back into his backpack. He left his pack on the beach, then he waded into the water.

"Great, huh?" called Annie.

"Yeah," Jack said as he dug his toes into the soft, gooey sand. Cool seawater lapped around his calves. He felt the warm sunshine on his face.

"Let's swim farther out," said Annie. "Maybe the secret of happiness is in the deep sea."

"How do we go down there without a submarine?" asked Jack.

"The wand," said Annie. "Maybe it will turn us into fish or something."

Jack closed his eyes and pictured the darkness of the deep filled with thousands of weird creatures. "But the wand can be used only after we've tried our hardest. I don't think we've done that yet," he said.

"Oh, right," said Annie. "Plus, it has to be for the good of others."

"So first we have to find some others," Jack said, his eyes still closed.

"Jack, you won't believe it," said Annie.

"What?" Jack asked dreamily.

"Take a look!" said Annie.

Jack sighed and opened his eyes. The mist had cleared a bit, and the day was becoming bright and hot.

"I think we just found the others!" said Annie. She pointed out to sea.

Jack shaded his eyes and squinted. Through the wavy sunlight, he saw a large wooden ship with three tall masts. "Whoa," he breathed. "That's a ship from a long time ago."

"Yeah. Remember when we ran into the pirate ship?" said Annie. "This ship looks the same, doesn't it?"

"Oh, no," said Jack. "Pirates *again*?"

"Look! A rowboat's leaving the ship," said Annie.

"Oh, man . . . ," said Jack.

"It's heading toward us," said Annie. "Just like that other time, remember? The pirates came ashore and chased us. Remember Pinky, Stinky, and Captain Bones?"

"Don't panic," said Jack, panicking. He splashed out of the water and ran up on the beach.

"Where should we go?" asked Annie, hurrying after him.

"To the tree house!" said Jack. He grabbed his backpack.

"But the pirates climbed up to the tree house," said Annie. "Pinky and Stinky found—"

"Forget Pinky and Stinky!" said Jack. "Let's just get out of here!"

Jack and Annie charged toward the sand dune. They raced up over the top and ran through the tall ferns and grass until they came to the rope ladder.

"Up, up!" cried Jack.

Jack and Annie climbed into the tree house. "Pull up the ladder!" said Jack. Together they hauled the rope ladder after them.

"Where's the Pennsylvania book?" said Jack. He looked around wildly for the book that always took them home. He grabbed it and found a picture of Frog Creek.

"Wait, wait! Don't make a wish yet!" said Annie. She was looking out the window. "I'm not so sure these guys are pirates."

Clutching the Pennsylvania book to his chest, Jack looked out the window with Annie. There were three men in the rowboat. The boat rode the top of a wave and came close to the beach.

Two of the men scrambled out and dragged the boat from the shallow water onto the sand. They both wore huge, bulky vests over white puffy-sleeved shirts. They wore round white hats and white pants rolled up to their knees.

"Those two don't look at all like Pinky and Stinky," said Annie.

"You're right," said Jack. "Pirates never wear such clean-looking clothes."

"And look at that third guy," said Annie.

The third man stepped out of the boat, carrying a butterfly net. He pulled off his bulky vest, revealing an old-fashioned suit and a bow tie.

"He *definitely* doesn't look like a pirate," said Annie.

"Yeah," said Jack. "He looks like he's never been on a boat before in his life."

As the two sailors pulled the rowboat farther onto the beach, the man in the bow tie picked up a stick. He started poking at clumps of seaweed.

"What's he doing?" asked Jack.

The man dropped his stick and picked up something small from the sand. He studied it for a moment. Then he knelt down, pulled a small book out of his pocket, and started to write.

"Who is he?" said Jack.

"I don't know," said Annie. "But one thing's for sure—pirates don't carry butterfly nets or write in notebooks."

"You're right," said Jack. He put down the Pennsylvania book. "So what's going on?"

"Let's go find out," said Annie. She dropped the rope ladder back to the ground and started down.

Jack grabbed his pack and hurried after her. Together they ran barefoot over the hot sand and through the feathery ferns. They climbed to the top of a sand dune and looked down. The three men were still at the edge of the water while the big ship drifted offshore.

"Hey, look. You can see the name of the ship," said Annie.

Jack peered through the haze and read on the side of the ship, HMS *Challenger*. "I'll look it up," he whispered. He pulled out their research book and searched the index. "It's here!" he whispered. He found the right page and read:

The HMS *Challenger* (HMS stands for Her Majesty's Ship) was a British navy vessel that served as the first dedicated scientific exploration ship in the history of the world.

"Oh, man," said Jack, looking up. "That is so cool."

"Yeah, read more," whispered Annie.

Jack read on:

> From 1872 to 1876, the HMS *Challenger* circled the globe, exploring the dark depths of the ocean. There were over 200 seamen and six scientists on board.

"So we landed in the 1870s," said Jack, looking up again.

"And that guy with the butterfly net must be one of the scientists," said Annie. "Come on, let's go meet him!"

Before Jack could tell her to wait, Annie darted down the sand dune. "Hey, guys!" she called. She waved her arms. "Hi!"

The three men whirled around. Their eyes grew wide and their mouths dropped open. They looked at Annie as if they were staring at a ghost.

CHAPTER THREE

A Creature Named Henry

Jack threw their book into his pack and quickly ran to join Annie. "Hi," he said to the three men.

"Don't be afraid," said Annie. "We come in peace."

The three men kept gawking. "Who—who *are* you?" one of the sailors sputtered.

Jack and Annie walked closer. "I'm Jack, and this is Annie," said Jack.

The man in the bow tie stepped forward. He had a long mustache and a big, friendly smile. "My name is Henry," he said. "I came ashore to look for rare butterflies, plants, and shells. But it seems I have found a rare creature called a Jack-and-Annie instead."

"And we've found a creature called a Henry," said Annie, giggling. "That's what we named a pteranodon when we went to the time of the dinosaurs."

"I beg your pardon?" said Henry.

"Uh . . . she's teasing," said Jack.

"What an unusual wit," said Henry, his eyes sparkling. "Well, you have not only found a Henry. You've also found a Joe and a Tommy, the two able seamen who rowed me here."

"Hi, Joe and Tommy," said Annie. She gave the two sailors a big smile.

But Joe and Tommy didn't smile back. They were both scowling. "Where are you from?" Joe asked suspiciously.

"Frog Creek, Pennsylvania," said Annie.

"Where is that?" asked Tommy.

"America," said Jack.

"How nice!" said Henry. "Why are you here?"

"We, uh . . . we're on vacation," said Annie.

"We're camped with our family back there some-where. . . ." She waved vaguely.

"Vacation?" said Henry.

"Our parents like to vacation in really out-of-the-way places," said Annie.

Henry chuckled. "Americans!"

"Are you a scientist from the HMS *Challenger*?" Jack said. He was eager to change the subject.

"Why, yes," said Henry. "I am one of the team trying to solve the riddles of the deep."

Jack loved the sound of that: *riddles of the deep*. "What kind of riddles have you solved so far?" he asked.

"Well, for one thing, we've learned that the ocean floor is absolutely teeming with life," said Henry.

"You didn't already know that?" asked Annie.

"We thought it was probably the case," said Henry. "But mind you, many people cannot imagine that life can exist in the icy darkness of the deep. In fact, some still believe there is no floor to the ocean at all! They think the sea goes down forever."

"Are you serious?" said Annie. "Ha. I guess you'll be letting them know that most of the ocean is not more than two miles deep. Of course, some ocean trenches are deeper than six miles. But—"

"Annie . . . ," said Jack.

"My, you know a lot about the sea," said Henry, looking at Annie with curiosity.

"Well, I know that mountain ranges and volcanoes are down there, too," said Annie.

Jack leaned in close to Annie. "Stop showing off," he said under his breath.

"Um . . . I mean *maybe,* just *maybe,*" Annie said to Henry. "Of course, I'm only guessing."

"You are a very good guesser," said Henry. "On our voyage, we've collected many volcanic rocks from the deep."

"Cool," said Annie. "How'd you get them? Mini-subs?"

"Mini-subs?" asked Henry.

"You know, they carry you down into the deep sea," said Annie.

"Annie!" said Jack between his teeth. He gave her a look that said *Just stop!* Jack was pretty sure mini-subs hadn't been invented by the early 1870s. He quickly changed the subject again. "And you study butterflies, too?" he said, pointing to Henry's net. "And seashells?"

"Indeed I do," said Henry. "In fact, I came ashore to search for a rare shell just now. And I think I may have found its cousin." He opened his book to a page that showed a pencil drawing of the shell.

"Would you like us to help you look for more?" asked Annie.

"Why, thank you," said Henry. "But I have quite successfully found what I came for. We'll be going back to the ship now."

"Oh, *please*, can we visit the HMS *Challenger*?" Annie blurted out.

"Out of the question," said the sailor named Joe.

"Well, I'm—" said Henry.

"Sir, the captain would *never* approve of bringing children on board," Tommy broke in. "It's absolutely against the rules."

Henry looked at Jack and Annie. Jack didn't want to break any rules, but at the same time, he really wanted to visit the ship. "We'd really like to learn more about sea exploration," he said. He gave the scientist a hopeful smile.

"We promise not to get in anyone's way," said Annie. "And our parents like us to learn new things."

Henry turned back to the two seamen. "Surely such bright and curious young people should be allowed to visit our ship," he said. "Since we'll be drifting and dredging in this area all day, we can return them to shore before nightfall."

Joe and Tommy frowned at each other. But Joe finally gave a quick nod.

"Yay!" Annie said.

"Thanks!" said Jack. "We promise we won't cause any trouble."

"See that you don't," said Henry with a smile. "Joe and Tommy, would you mind lending our two visitors your life preservers?"

"Never fit 'em, sir," said Joe.

"Well, we must do what we can to keep them safe," said Henry.

The two seamen grudgingly handed Jack and Annie their bulky vests.

So these are old-fashioned life preservers! thought Jack. The vests were made of blocks of cork tied together. Even though Jack buckled his tightly, it hung low on his body, almost slipping off.

"I'm afraid they are rather big," said Henry, "but still they might save you should we capsize."

"Don't worry," said Annie. "We're really good swimmers."

"We should go now, sir," Joe said impatiently.

"Yes, yes," Henry said. "Let us be off!"

Joe and Tommy pushed the rowboat into the shallow water. While Jack and Annie had been talking with Henry, the water had turned choppy. Dark gray clouds had rolled in, hiding the sun.

"Climb in after me!" Henry told Jack and Annie, and they followed him into the rowboat.

Jack's backpack wouldn't fit over his life jacket. So he clutched the pack to his chest as Joe and Tommy pushed the boat farther into the ocean. The sailors jumped in, picked up their oars, and began rowing back to the ship.

CHAPTER FOUR

Off the Ship!

"The wind's against us!" Joe said as he and Tommy rowed.

Even after the boat moved past the breakers, it kept bouncing up and down on the swell of the waves. Water splashed over the sides and soaked Jack's clothes. But Jack wasn't worried about the wind or water. He was worried about being sea-sick, because waves of nausea had started to come over him.

"Sorry it's a bit of tough going!" Henry said.

"We can take it!" Annie said.

We hope, thought Jack. The last thing he wanted to do was throw up, especially in front of Joe and Tommy!

"We should get back just in time to see the men haul up this morning's catch!" said Henry.

"This is so much fun!" said Annie, her eyes shining as the little rowboat bobbed up and down.

Jack wasn't having any fun at all. To keep from being sick, he gripped his backpack, closed his eyes, and gritted his teeth.

"Every day we make new discoveries," said Henry. "Off the coast of Argentina, we found over one hundred new species! Giant worms several feet long! Shrimp the size of lobsters! Caught them in our nets, didn't we, Joe?"

"Aye," said Joe as he pulled on the oars. "But the creature that's never been caught is the one these mates should be worried about!"

"What creature is that?" asked Annie.

"The great monster," answered Tommy.

Jack opened his eyes. "What? You mean like a shark?" he asked.

"No, no, lad, 'tis much worse than any shark, even the twenty-foot tiger shark that's been following us," said Tommy. The sailor blinked nervously.

Whoa, twenty-foot tiger shark?! thought Jack. He looked at the dark water for a shark fin.

"Aye! This monster's much bigger than *any* shark!" shouted Joe. "They say it looks like a cross between a dragon and a gigantic starfish."

"Nay, more like a floating nest of snakes, mate," said Tommy with a shudder. "They say it'll curl around your body and strangle you to death!"

"A floating nest of snakes?" Annie asked.

Jack gulped. He turned to Henry. "Have *you* seen the monster?" he asked the scientist.

Henry shook his head. "I've never seen it," he said. "But a few of our crewmen claim to have glimpsed something monstrous in these waters just yesterday."

"Don't be scared, mates!" said Joe. "If we see a monster, we'll hurl our harpoons at 'im!"

"We'll shoot 'im with our cannons!" said Tommy. He and Joe laughed loudly.

Maybe the sailors on the ship are just trying to scare the scientists, Jack thought hopefully. Why else would they be laughing?

When they reached the HMS *Challenger,* the rowboat drew alongside the big ship, rocking on the water. Jack gripped his pack tighter as more waves of seasickness washed over him.

"You go first, mate!" Joe said to Jack. "You're looking a bit green."

Clutching his pack under one arm, Jack grabbed the sides of the ladder. He held on tightly and climbed from the wooden hull of the ship up to the top deck. Annie came after him, then Henry, Joe, and Tommy. When they were all on the deck, the two seamen hauled up the rowboat.

Jack took a long, deep breath. Though the large ship rocked in the wind, it wasn't nearly as bad as the small rowboat's movement on the waves. Looking around the deck, Jack saw teams of sailors working. Some were coiling thick ropes. Others were hauling up strange-looking buckets.

Jack turned to ask Henry what the sailors were doing. But Henry was staring at a tall man in a white uniform and a heavyset older man in a dark suit who were walking briskly toward them. The two men were frowning.

"Oh, no," murmured Henry. "Prepare to meet thy doom."

"Who are they?" asked Annie.

Before Henry could answer, the man in white shouted, "What have you done *this* time, Mr. Moseley?"

Jack moved closer to Annie. He clutched his pack to his life vest.

"Well, Captain, I—" started Henry.

"Goodness, what have you brought up from

the sea now, Henry?" the portly man asked. "A four-legged, four-armed creature of the deep?"

"Yes, Professor. It's a Jack-and-Annie from America," said Henry. "I found the creature vacationing on the island."

The portly man smiled. "Oh, I see. I thought perhaps it was the monster that was sighted by some of the men yesterday."

The monster again! thought Jack.

"This ship is *not* a place for children, Mr. Moseley," the captain said gruffly.

"Yes, I know, sir," said Henry. "But these two are extraordinary. They hardly seem like children at all. They're quite independent and have great knowledge of the sea. I thought it might be permissible to bring them aboard for the afternoon and then return them to shore."

"I'm afraid it goes against all the ship's rules," said the captain.

"It's not Henry's fault, Captain," Annie piped up. "We begged him to let us visit your ship."

"Ah, did you now?" the portly man asked, his eyes twinkling. "Why is that?"

"We love the ocean!" said Annie.

"And we'd really like to learn more about sea exploration, sir," said Jack.

"Well, you've come to the right place!" said the man. "Allow me to introduce myself. I am Professor Thomson, the scientific director of the *Challenger.*"

"The professor is one of the world's most renowned experts on the ocean," said Henry.

"Wow," said Annie.

"Well, I don't know about *that,*" the professor said modestly. But he put his thumbs in his vest and began speaking as if he were giving a lecture. "Since the beginning of time, the secrets of the deep have been hidden from us. But now, with our expedition, we have learned many things."

"Like what?" asked Jack.

"We have used miles and miles of steel wire to measure the depth of the sea," said the professor.

"We have lowered thermometers to measure temperatures in the deep. But perhaps most important of all, we are learning about the amazing creatures who live in the dark regions far beneath the ocean waves—"

"That is all well and good, Professor," the captain broke in. "But I want these children off this ship immediately! Before the weather gets worse. Do you hear, Mr. Moseley? Off the ship!"

CHAPTER FIVE

Ooze

The captain turned and strode away.

"Sorry, friends," Henry said to Jack and Annie. "But the captain's in charge." He looked around. "I see Joe and Tommy are helping the men bring up the catch now. As soon as they are free, I will ask them to take you back to shore. I am very sorry."

"That's okay," said Annie. "You did what you could."

"Before you young people leave, perhaps you would like to see today's specimens?" asked the professor.

"Sure!" said Jack and Annie together.

"Then come along!" said the professor. "Every single day we make new discoveries!"

Hurrying with Annie across the deck, Jack couldn't wait to see what had just been brought up from the deep. They followed Henry and the professor to a team of sailors pulling up large nets. The nets were shaped like giant bags with mops attached to the bottom.

"What are those mops for?" asked Annie.

"They sweep up sea animals from the floor of the ocean," explained Henry.

"We pull them from pitch-darkness into the light of day," said the professor.

"That must scare them!" said Annie.

But the professor didn't seem to hear her. "Over the years, we've hauled up tens of thousands of specimens!" he said.

As the sailors dumped the bags onto the deck, Jack saw mostly mud. But lying in the mud were tiny, squirmy pink and yellow fish and fiery orange sea stars.

"No monsters there, huh?" asked Annie.

The professor looked at her. "Not today, my dear," he said.

"I was just kidding," said Annie. "Do you believe in monsters?"

"Oh. Well . . ." The professor looked serious. "The sea is very deep, my dear. It covers nearly three-quarters of the world. So I say to myself, 'Might it not indeed hold many mysterious creatures, including monsters?'"

Good point, thought Jack.

"But don't be afraid, children!" said the professor. "Someday we'll catch all the monsters and study them! We will conquer our fears through knowledge! Won't we, Henry?"

"Yes, sir," said Henry.

"Conquer our fears through knowledge!" The professor repeated his thought with enthusiasm. "I shall add that to my lectures."

Low thunder rolled in the sky.

Jack looked up. Black clouds hovered overhead. A strong gust of wind swept over the deck.

"Attention!" the captain shouted, heading toward them. "A squall is headed our way! For now, take the children below to the main deck."

"Yes, sir!" said Henry. He smiled at Jack and Annie. "Well, friends, I suppose you get to stay with us a while longer, after all."

"Yay!" Annie said softly.

"Only those on watch stay on deck!" the captain shouted to his crew. "Everyone else get below."

Henry led Jack and Annie away just as the rain began to pour down. Water dripped from Jack's hair and backpack and life vest as he and Annie followed Henry down a steep flight of stairs to a dimly lit hallway.

"Our ship was converted from a war vessel to a ship of sea laboratories," Henry said. "The navy removed sixteen of the eighteen guns on board to make room for them. Would you like to see mine?"

"Oh, yes!" said Jack. He couldn't wait to see an actual sea laboratory.

"Follow me." Henry unlocked a door and

showed Jack and Annie into a large, dim room. There was a small skylight overhead. Rain pounded against the glass.

Henry struck a match and lit a couple of oil lamps. Shadows danced around the room.

Jack smiled and let out a deep sigh. He loved the sea lab. Shelves were lined with hundreds of different-size bottles. The bottles were filled with floating blobs. In the middle of the room was a wooden table. It held maps, rulers, thermometers, bowls with gooey-looking stuff, and a big microscope.

Henry pointed at the microscope. "Would you like to see something remarkable?" he asked.

"Oh, yes!" said Annie. She peered through the eyepiece. "Whoa—that's amazing," she breathed.

"Let me see," said Jack. He put his backpack down on the table and looked in the microscope. He saw the tiny skeleton of a sea horse. "Cool . . . ," he said.

"That sea horse is no bigger than a grain of

sugar," said Henry. "But of course I'm fascinated by larger creatures as well. Why, just yesterday I spent several hours studying the ear bone of a dolphin and the tooth of a shark."

"And what's in all those bottles?" asked Annie. She pointed at the rows and rows of bottles on Henry's shelves.

"Many curiosities," said the scientist. "That large one, for instance, holds a creature that looks like a giant sock. Some call it a blubber fish. But it's not a fish at all! It is made up of millions of tiny sea creatures."

"Eww," said Annie.

"And there's a rare sea slug," said Henry. He pointed to a bright yellow blob floating in a clear liquid.

"Nice color," said Jack.

"We study whatever we bring up from the deep," said Henry. "We measure the specimens and identify them. Then we preserve them in bottles of alcohol and label the bottles."

"So all those bottles are full of dead sea creatures?" said Annie.

"Oh, no. Many bottles are simply filled with ooze from the bottom of the sea," said Henry.

"Ooze?" said Jack.

"The official name for mud," said Henry, smiling. "Here, feel it." Henry picked up one of the plates on the table and held it out to Jack and Annie. They rubbed the sticky, wet mud between their fingers.

"*Ooze* is a good name for it," said Jack.

Henry gave them a cloth to wipe their hands.

Then he picked up a large book from the table. "And here is the notebook where I transfer my drawings of natural history specimens," he said. He opened the book. Inside were beautiful watercolors of shells, plants, and butterflies.

"These are great," said Jack. Henry's notebook reminded him of the notebooks he'd seen in Leonardo da Vinci's studio.

"This is beautiful," said Annie. She reached across Henry's table and picked up a gleaming, round seashell. The shell was white with curved reddish brown lines.

"Yes," Henry said softly. "My nautilus shell."

"Is this one of your specimens?" asked Annie.

"No," said Henry. "I don't consider that a specimen. It's more like a treasure. I'm afraid I grew quite fond of the little creature who once lived inside that shell."

"What did he do?" asked Annie.

"Oh, he just swam around a small tub I had for him," said Henry. "But he moved backwards.

Rather funny. He filled himself with water and then squirted it out—all over me!" Henry smiled. "I was quite sad when he died. I wished I had returned him to the sea." Henry put the shell down and let out a quiet sigh. "Silly to think that way, I know."

"Not silly at all," said Annie.

The ship's bell rang.

"Ah, time to go," said Henry. "The captain runs a tight ship. It's against the rules to be late. So let us be off to the wardroom."

"What's the wardroom?" Jack asked.

"That's where the scientists and naval officers eat," said Henry.

"Eat?" Jack said weakly. The thought of food made him feel queasy again.

"Yes," said Henry. He blew out the two oil lamps. "Come along! You must join us! It's lunchtime!"

CHAPTER SIX

Pea Soup

Henry led Jack and Annie out of the sea lab, locking the door behind them. Then he led the way through the hall and down another flight of steep steps. In the faint light of the lower deck, Jack saw naval officers and scientists streaming through a door ahead. He, Annie, and Henry lined up behind them and filed into the ward-room.

Still wearing their bulky life vests, Jack and Annie sat awkwardly on a long bench in front of a table. Many of the men stared at them with curiosity. The professor smiled, but the captain did not look happy.

"I thought our friends might join us for lunch, sir," Henry said to the captain. "I promise they will return to shore after the storm."

"Very well," said the captain. "*Immediately* after the storm."

"Aye, aye, sir," said Henry. He turned to the other officers at the table. "Gentlemen, may I introduce Annie and Jack from America. They are adventurous travelers."

"Hi," murmured Jack and Annie.

The officers and scientists nodded politely.

Sailors in white uniforms acted as waiters, bringing plates and cups to the table. "What are we having for lunch?" Annie whispered to Henry.

"The usual," said Henry, sighing. "Salted meat, pickles, dried biscuits."

This is not good, thought Jack. He was right. When he was served, he could hardly look at his food, much less eat it. He was thirsty, though. So he reached for his cup and took a long sip of water.

Jack immediately spit the liquid back into his cup. It was unbelievably sour! He gagged and coughed. When he looked up, everyone was staring at him, including the captain. "Excuse me," Jack said, wiping his mouth. His face felt hot from embarrassment.

"You just guzzled your lime juice, lad," said the professor. "Most of us take it in small sips."

"Lime juice?" asked Annie. "Why?"

"It prevents scurvy," said the Professor. "Every day we all drink a cup of lime juice for vitamin C. Otherwise, we'd get sores and rotten teeth."

"Yuck," said Annie.

Henry smiled. "You won't get scurvy if you eat fruits and vegetables," he said. "But it is hard to keep vegetables and fruits fresh on board a ship."

Jack couldn't think about eating or drinking

anything at the moment. All of it—especially the pickles—made him feel even queasier. The rolling of the ship didn't help, either. "The waves seem to be getting worse," he said to Henry.

"They do indeed," said Henry. He turned and looked out a small, round window. "Can't see a thing. It's as thick as pea soup out there."

Oh, no, Jack groaned to himself. *Please don't talk about pea soup.*

The ship lurched. Cups and plates slid across the table and crashed to the floor. Annie grabbed Jack as the ship rocked wildly.

"Steady as she goes!" said the captain.

"It seems the storm is fully upon us," said the professor.

The ship lurched again. More cups and plates slid off the table. Jack and Annie almost slid off their chairs. But without any sign of nervousness, the officers and scientists stood up and hurried out of the room, as if they knew just what to do in bad weather.

"I'll take you down to the hold," Henry said to Jack and Annie. "We'll wait there until the waves calm down."

The ship pitched violently as they stood up from the table. Holding on to the back of their life

vests, Henry steered Jack and Annie out of the wardroom. Jack nearly slipped on the wet floor. His bare feet crushed some soggy biscuits and pickles. He tried not to think about it.

Out in the dark hall, the wind howled down the stairwell from the top deck, spraying them all with ocean foam.

"I must go secure my lab," Henry shouted to Jack and Annie. He pointed to the stairs. "Go down one more flight! I'll join you when I can!"

"We'll come with you!" said Annie.

"'Tis better to be safe!" said Henry. "Follow the others quickly! I'll come soon!" Henry unlocked the door to his lab and disappeared inside.

"Come on, let's go down!" said Jack. He grabbed Annie's hand and pulled her toward the stairwell. Officers and sailors were all heading down the steps ahead of them.

Just as Jack and Annie started down, the ship lurched again. Jack's stomach lurched with it. He covered his mouth. *I am definitely going to be sick!* he thought. He really didn't want to throw up on the stairs—or in front of the captain and the others!

"You go down! I'll be right there!" Jack shouted to Annie.

"Why? Where are you going?" Annie yelled.

"Just go down!" said Jack. Then he whirled around and charged up two flights of steep steps to the top deck.

When Jack stepped onto the deck, the rain was pounding. The wind was howling. The waves looked like dark mountains. Sea foam was blowing everywhere.

Jack knew at once he'd made a mistake. *Better to be embarrassed than drown!* he thought. Just as he turned to go back down the steps, Annie burst onto the deck.

"Jack!" she cried. "What are you doing?"

Jack forgot all about throwing up. "I made a mistake!" he shouted. "We shouldn't be up here! Go down! I'm coming with you! We have to go back down!" He pushed Annie toward the stairwell.

A giant wave crashed over the side of the

ship. Jack fell and slid across the foam-covered deck. It was impossible to see anything. The wind was screaming. Jack tried to stand, but wearing his clumsy life vest, he couldn't get back on his feet.

Jack finally hauled himself up. But just as he did, another giant wave broke over the side of the ship! The ship rolled again, and Jack fell to his knees. Another wave crashed over the deck. Jack was swept up by the foamy water—and tossed overboard into the churning sea!

CHAPTER SEVEN

Help!

Jack plunged down into the sea. The water was freezing cold. He bobbed back up to the surface, choking and coughing. The life vest kept Jack afloat, but the waves kept hammering him.

"Help!" Jack shouted. Thoughts of the twenty-foot tiger shark and the mysterious monster shot through his mind. "Help! Help!" he screamed.

Jack heard someone else screaming, "Help!" It was Annie! She'd been washed off the ship, too!

Jack flailed his arms and kicked his legs, trying to get to Annie. A wave lifted her up and tossed her toward him. But just as Jack reached for her hand, another wave pushed her past him, out of reach.

"The wand, Jack!" Annie shouted. "Use the wand!"

The wand! Jack thought. *The Wand of Dianthus!* Where was it? In his backpack! He didn't have his backpack! Where was his backpack?

"Jack! The wand!" Annie yelled.

"I don't have it!" Jack shouted. His voice was lost in the roar of the storm. Jack kept flailing and kicking, trying to reach Annie again.

Jack felt his cork life vest coming loose. Another wave crashed over him, and one side of the vest slipped off his arm!

Jack clutched the vest, trying to keep it on. But the waters kept pulling and tugging. The sea itself now seemed like a monster!

As Jack desperately fought the water, he saw another life vest floating free on the waves. It was Annie's!

Where was she?

"Annie!" Jack screamed. As he looked around, he lost his fight with the sea—a wave washed his vest right off him! Then another wave crashed down on his head and pushed him down into the deep.

Jack held his breath as he plunged through the black water. He thrashed his arms and kicked his legs, trying to get back to the surface. His head popped above the waves, and he took one deep gulp of air before another wave washed over him and he went under again.

Jack kept kicking and trying to swim, but the fight to get back to the surface was too great. Just when he was about to run out of air, he felt something curl around his waist. Then he felt himself being lifted toward the surface!

Jack's head popped above the water again. He

opened his mouth and gasped for air. The waves were swirling and foamy, but Jack kept his head above them. Something around his waist was holding him up.

Jack couldn't think at first. He was trying too hard to breathe. But then he saw something spreading across the water near him. It looked like a giant gray umbrella with dark spots all over it.

Rising from the center of the umbrella was a huge, rounded head! It had yellow eyes with black pupils. Stretching out from the umbrella were tentacles—*lots* of tentacles, all connected by a thick web, with double rows of suckers on each one.

A giant octopus! Jack thought with horror. It was much bigger than the octopus they'd seen a long time ago. And this time, a tentacle of the huge creature was curling around his waist!

"Help!" Jack shrieked. He tried to pull himself free from the thick, rubbery arm.

The giant octopus held him tightly. Jack looked around wildly. Where was Annie?

"Jack!" Annie shouted.

Jack saw her. One of the octopus tentacles had lifted Annie above the surface of the water, too.

Jack's relief at seeing Annie was matched by his terror. "We're caught!" he cried. "Try to escape!"

Jack kept trying to break free from the huge tentacle. But the more he fought, the tighter the grip of the octopus became.

"Don't fight him, Jack!" Annie yelled. "He's rescuing us!"

Jack couldn't think straight. Was she crazy? "He'll strangle us and pull us back under!" he shouted. "We *have* to fight him!"

"No!" shouted Annie. "You're wrong! Can't you see? He's saving us from drowning!"

He is? thought Jack.

Jack tried not to panic. The octopus arm around his middle felt firm, but he could tell that it wasn't trying to strangle him. It actually felt like it was hugging him, circling him like an inner tube, holding him above the water.

Jack saw the creature's huge yellow eyes fixed on him. As Jack stared back into his eyes, he knew what Annie was saying was true. The creature wasn't trying to hurt him. Instead, the octopus looked concerned. He looked curious, too, and even a little shy.

Staring back into the eyes of the octopus, Jack found himself smiling. As he and Annie kept bobbing up and down in the arms of the octopus, all of Jack's fear vanished. This was the weirdest rescue he'd ever experienced.

"Hi, you," Annie said to the octopus. "We come in peace."

Jack felt so dazed he started laughing. Annie laughed, too. Even the octopus looked amused.

Their laughter was interrupted by the blare of a horn. Jack heard men shrieking and shouting. He looked up and saw the HMS *Challenger* heading toward them.

CHAPTER EIGHT

Monster of the Deep

Sailors were on the top deck. They were yelling and pointing.

The giant octopus loosened his hold on Jack and Annie.

"The ship!" Jack gurgled before slipping under the water. His head popped back up. "Swim to the ship!" he shouted to Annie.

Jack and Annie started swimming. The sky was still covered with clouds and the sea was still rough. But arm over arm, they swam until they got close to the ladder on the side of the ship.

"Ahoy!" someone shouted from above. Jack looked up and saw Henry and the professor standing at the top of the ladder.

"Climb up!" yelled Henry.

"Hurry, children! Hurry!" cried the professor. "Before it comes back!"

Jack swam as fast as he could to the ladder. He and Annie got there at the same time. They pulled themselves onto the ladder and climbed. When they reached the top, Henry and the professor helped them onto the deck. Henry wrapped wool blankets around them.

"Thank goodness you are saved!" said the professor.

"I thought you were below in the hold!" said Henry. "How did you end up in the water?"

"The storm . . . the waves . . . ," gasped Jack, shivering.

"The waves threw us overboard," said Annie.

"Why were you up on deck?" said Henry.

"I was—I was seasick!" said Jack.

"I followed Jack, and big waves came crashing down and washed us into the water!" said Annie.

"Our life vests saved us at first," said Jack. "But then they came off!"

"Then the octopus saved us," said Annie.

"That monster *saved* you?" asked the professor.

"No, no, *not* a monster," said Jack, "a giant octopus!"

"Yes, the monster of the deep! I do not think it saved you, boy," said the professor. "It is a miracle it did not eat you and your sister alive!"

"No, no, he's—he's *not* a monster. He didn't try to do any of that—" said Jack.

"He *did* save us!" said Annie. "He held us up above the water."

"*Really!*" said Jack. "He kept us from drowning. Then he got scared away by the ship."

"We didn't even thank him, Jack," said Annie. "We didn't say good-bye."

Jack and Annie looked back at the water.

"Hey, what's going on over there?" said Annie. She pointed to the rear of the ship. Sailors were facing the sea, yelling and shouting.

"What are they yelling at?" Annie asked.

Jack and Annie threw off their blankets and took off across the deck. They saw Joe and Tommy standing at the edge of the crowd.

"What are they doing?" Annie yelled. "What's going on?"

"They snared it in the net!" shouted Tommy.

"We've caught the beast at last!" shouted Joe.

"Caught it?" Annie looked at Jack.

"Come on!" Jack cried. He and Annie pushed their way through the crowd.

"Children, stop!" the professor shouted, hurrying after them. "Don't get in the way!"

But Jack and Annie squeezed through the crowd of sailors and scientists until they got to the railing of the ship. They looked down.

The giant octopus was tangled in a net. His arms were churning the seawater into foam.

His body had turned bright red. A cloud of dark ink billowed around him.

"You're hurting him!" yelled Annie. "Leave him alone!"

"Move away!" yelled a sailor.

Some of the sailors were yelling mean things at the octopus. Others seemed terrified. Even the captain was caught up in the panic. "Stand back!" he shouted. "It could be powerful enough to sink the ship!"

"That's crazy!" yelled Jack. "Leave him alone!"

"Its tentacles are as hard as steel!" shouted one of the sailors.

"No, they're not!" cried Annie. "They're soft! They saved us from drowning!"

But everyone kept shouting:

"Hungry for human flesh!"

"Devour a man in one bite!"

"Thirsty for blood!"

"He's not *any* of those things!" yelled Annie.

"Throw the harpoons!" yelled a sailor.

"Get your axes, swords, and knives!" yelled another.

"Ready the guns!" said the captain.

"No!" screamed Annie.

"No!" roared Jack.

"The children are right!" shouted the professor. He and Henry had squeezed through the crowd, too. They were standing behind Jack and Annie.

Jack felt a rush of relief. "The professor says we're right!" yelled Annie.

"Do not destroy it, Captain!" roared the professor. "Haul it on board!"

"On board?" said Jack.

"Capture it alive and whole!" said the professor. His eyes gleamed. "So we can study it!"

"No, no, let him go," said Jack. "Just let him swim away and be free!"

"Please!" screamed Annie. "Let him go!"

But neither the professor nor the captain seemed to hear Jack and Annie. They were too busy arguing over what to do with the giant octopus.

"We must kill it, Professor!" said the captain. "It could grab the hull and drag the ship down to the bottom!"

"But science needs it alive!" said the professor. "At least till we have examined it!"

By now the octopus had gathered his long arms around himself, as if for protection.

Annie burst into tears. "Henry, help him!" she sobbed. "Don't let them kill him! Or capture him!"

Henry looked upset, too. "Excuse me, sirs!" he shouted. "Excuse me! The girl is right! We should let him go!"

But no one listened to Henry, either.

"Jack!" cried Annie. She grabbed Jack. Tears were streaming down her cheeks. "Save him! We have to save him!"

"What can we do? We've tried everything!" said Jack.

Then he remembered. His own words helped him remember. And Jack knew *exactly* what to do.

CHAPTER NINE

Think! Think!

"Where's my backpack?" Jack yelled to Annie.

"What?" Annie said.

"My backpack!" said Jack.

"Don't worry about that now," said Annie. "We have to—"

"The wand! The wand!" Jack interrupted her.

"Oh!" said Annie. "The wand!"

"We have to find my pack! Fast!" said Jack.

Jack and Annie pushed past the sailors crowding the railing. They ran across the deck.

"Did you bring it in the rowboat?" yelled Annie.

"Yes! No! I don't know!" said Jack. "I can't remember!"

"Think! Think!" said Annie.

Jack tried to think as they ran around the upper deck of the ship. *Did I have it in the rowboat? What happened in the rowboat? I felt sick in the rowboat! I hugged my backpack in the rowboat!*

"I remember!" Jack shouted. "I was holding on to it when we first came aboard!"

"Then it's here somewhere!" said Annie.

"The wardroom!" said Jack.

"Hurry!" cried Annie.

Jack and Annie raced down two flights of steps. They looked in the wardroom. Jack's pack wasn't there!

"Henry's lab!" said Annie.

"Yes! Yes! It's in there!" Jack cried. "I remember now! I left it on the table. I put it down when I looked through the microscope!"

Jack and Annie ran up one flight of steps to

Henry's lab. They tried to open the door, but it was locked!

"We need Henry!" said Jack.

"We don't have time!" said Annie.

"We don't have a choice!" said Jack.

Jack and Annie charged back up the stairs to the upper deck.

The crew was still gathered at the end of the deck, yelling and shrieking about the octopus.

Henry was coming toward them!

"Henry, help us!" said Annie. She raced to Henry and grabbed him by the arm. She pulled him toward the stairs. "You have to unlock your lab! We have to get Jack's pack! It's life or death! Hurry, *hurry!*"

"Why? What?" sputtered Henry.

"We'll explain later!" said Jack.

"Just hurry!" said Annie.

Henry looked baffled, but he walked quickly and led Jack and Annie down the stairs. They nearly pushed him across the hall toward his lab.

The scientist pulled out his key and unlocked the door.

Jack and Annie burst into the lab. "Yay!" said Annie. Jack's pack was on the table!

Jack grabbed it and tore it open. He pulled out the Wand of Dianthus. The silver spiraled wand gleamed in the dim light of the room.

"What is that?" asked Henry.

"We'll explain later!" said Annie.

"Come on, let's go back up!" said Jack.

"No, we don't have time!" cried Annie. "Use it now, Jack! Say something now! Before they hurt him!"

Jack held up the wand.

"Five words!" said Annie.

"I know," said Jack. But what five words? This was their only chance!

"Hurry!" said Annie.

"I am!" said Jack. "But we can't just save him this one time. We have to make sure the ship never, ever tries to hurt him or others like him again."

Jack closed his eyes. He pictured the giant octopus . . . his umbrella-like body and long tentacles, the gaze of his yellow eyes—a gaze that had curiosity and shyness.

Jack thought of the sheer wonder of the octopus's existence. The giant sea animal was incredibly amazing. He was like a miracle.

Jack wished he and Annie could explain the miracle of the octopus to everyone. But no one would listen to them. Unless—

"Hurry, Jack! Say the words!" said Annie.

"Make them hear the truth!" The words had burst out of Jack.

"What?" said Annie.

"Make—them—hear—the—truth!" said Jack, his eyes still shut tight. "That's my wish. Make all the guys upstairs hear the truth about the octopus."

"What are you talking about?" said Henry. "What is that stick you're waving?"

Jack opened his eyes. He shook his head at Annie. But she didn't see him.

"It's a magic wand!" Annie said to Henry.

"Actually—" said Jack, trying to think of something else to say.

"Oh, oh, yes, I see," said Henry. He smiled sadly. "You're pretending, like children."

"We *are* children!" said Annie. "Come on, Jack. Let's go tell them the truth!"

CHAPTER TEN

The Heart of the Ocean

Jack put the wand back in his pack. Then he and Annie charged out of the lab, with Henry behind them.

The three of them climbed back up the stairs. When they stepped onto the top deck, they heard the sailors still shouting and yelling. Jack and Annie raced across the deck. They pushed through the crowd until they got to the railing.

The octopus was still in the net, bright red and hiding his head in fear. The sailors had gathered weapons. Some were aiming harpoons.

Others stood by with knives. Some pointed pistols.

"Stop!" cried Annie.

"Stand back!" the captain yelled at her.

"You must bring it up alive!" begged the professor. "I beg you to let me examine it before you slay it, Captain!"

But before the captain could answer, someone hurled a harpoon at the creature. It missed and landed in the water with a splash.

"No!" yelled Annie.

"Listen to us!" Jack yelled in his loudest voice. "You have to hear the truth!" He stood up on the bottom rung of the ship's railing so everyone could hear him. "Don't touch him!" he shouted. "He's not going to hurt you! He deserves to live peacefully in the sea! He's a miracle of nature!"

But no one was listening to Jack. No one even turned to look at him.

"Stop! Hear us!" said Annie. "We speak the truth! Leave him alone!"

"Remove the children!" the captain roared again. "Now!"

Tommy and Joe grabbed Jack and Annie.

"Let us go! We have to talk to them!" yelled Annie, kicking and flailing. She and Jack broke loose from the sailors.

"She's right! They have to hear the truth!" yelled Jack, running toward the railing. "He's okay where he is! He's different from people, but he's a miracle!"

Again, no one seemed to hear him.

"The magic's not working!" Annie cried to Jack.

"I know!" said Jack. He was desperate. No one was hearing the truth! *What was wrong?* He and Annie had followed the rules: They were trying to help others, not themselves. They had tried their hardest first. And Jack had used only five words.

"Look!" a sailor shrieked. "Look at the monster!"

Jack and Annie looked back at the water.

The giant octopus had uncovered his head and raised it out of the water. "LEHHHHHHHH!" The sound was breathy and whispery, as if it came from the wind.

The members of the crew lowered their weapons and stepped back in awe. "It—it speaks!" shouted a sailor.

"MEEEEEEEEEEE!" The sound was wild and shrill, as if it came from a deep forest.

"GOOOOOOOOO!" The sound was hollow and haunted, as if it came from an ancient gong or bell or drum.

"HOOOOOOOOME!" The sound was unbearably sad, as if it came from the heart of the ocean.

"IMMMMMNOOOOOMONNNSTERRR!" The octopus fell back into the water. All the seamen and scientists stared in wonder and terror.

Then Annie's voice rang through the silence. "Did you hear him? He said, 'Let me go home. I'm no monster.'"

The crew looked at each other in shock.

"That's what 'e said. I heard it," one man said. "Heard it with my own ears."

"I heard it, too!" said another.

"Me too!" said another.

"It's a sign," said a sailor. "We can't hurt 'im—"

"Or any other like 'im!" said another.

All eyes turned to the captain. He stood still for a moment, staring down at the giant octopus in the net. The captain looked at the professor. The professor seemed stunned. He opened his mouth, but no words came out.

The captain looked at Jack and Annie. "Please hear him," Annie said. "He told you the truth."

The captain stared at the octopus for a long moment. Then he raised his hand. "Free him," he said softly.

The sailors slowly put down their harpoons, axes, pistols, and ropes.

"Sir, I request permission to cut the creature from the net," Henry said to the captain.

The captain nodded. "Permission granted, Mr. Moseley," said the captain.

"Help me," Henry said to Jack and Annie.

"Sure!" said Jack.

"We'll come, too, mate," said Joe.

Joe and Tommy hurried after Henry, Jack, and Annie to a row of small boats on the deck. The sailors lowered one of the boats down to the surface of the water. Then Jack, Annie, Joe, Tommy, and Henry all climbed down the ladder and stepped inside.

Everyone else watched from the deck. Joe and Tommy rowed along the side of the ship until they came to the spot where the giant octopus was trapped. The two sailors held the boat steady with their oars. "Grab the net," Henry said to Jack and Annie.

Jack reached out and grabbed a corner of the net. Annie helped him pull it out of the water. Henry used a big knife to slice through the thick rope strands.

Even though the rowboat rocked violently, Jack didn't feel sick at all.

Jack, Annie, and Henry pulled the torn net into the small boat. Jack kept staring at the octopus. He looked back at all of them with his great

eyes, his tentacles spread about him like a giant flower. His fierce red color had changed back to gray.

"Good-bye, you," Annie said softly. "Go home now."

The octopus lifted two of his tentacles as if to wave good-bye. Then he slipped under the surface of the water and vanished.

CHAPTER ELEVEN

Good-bye, Mates

Jack looked up. The captain, the professor, and the crew members were all gazing silently down at the water.

Henry gave the captain a salute. The captain saluted back. Then everyone on board clapped and shouted.

Overhead the clouds had disappeared, as if a curtain had been pulled away from the sky. Pink and red swirls of light streaked the blue.

The cheering died down. "Let us disturb these waters no more!" commanded the captain.

"Unfurl the sails! Get the steam up in the boilers!"

Henry turned to Jack and Annie. "While they prepare the ship, shall we return you to shore?" he asked.

"Yes, please," said Annie.

Jack just nodded. He was totally exhausted.

As Joe and Tommy started rowing back toward land, the wind shifted and died down to a breeze.

"I predict a fine, clear night tonight," said Tommy.

"And tomorrow, too," said Joe. "The wind should be brisk."

"A good time to sail," said Tommy.

When they drew close to shore, Tommy and Joe both jumped out of the boat. Splashing through the shallows, they pulled the boat up onto the beach. Jack and Annie hopped out. Henry climbed out after them.

"Thanks!" Jack said to the sailors.

Henry walked with Annie and Jack up to the dunes. "Are you sure you'll be all right?" he asked. "What will you do when night comes on?"

"Don't worry," said Jack. "We'll get back to our parents before dark."

"Lucky you," Henry said wistfully. "I wish I could be back to my own family before dark."

"I hope you keep having a good voyage," said Annie.

"And I hope you learn a lot," said Jack. "Bye."

"Wait, before you go—" said Henry. "I want to give you something." Henry reached into the pocket of his vest and took out the beautiful nautilus shell. "The real reason I ran into my lab when the storm came was to get this," he said. "I didn't want to risk losing it. But now I would like to give it to you."

"Oh, no, Henry. You love it. You keep it," said Annie.

"I do love it," said Henry. "But I want you two to have it. Today you taught me—no, you taught

all of us—an important lesson. It is a dark day in the deep sea when we cause innocent creatures to suffer. The professor said we can conquer our fears through knowledge. But you taught us that our fears can best be conquered through compassion. Even we scientists must never forget to have compassion for all living creatures. My compassion for the little creature that once lived in this shell made me very happy."

Oh, man! thought Jack. *That's the secret!*

Henry held out the gleaming nautilus shell, and Annie took it from him. "Thanks, Henry," said Annie. "We promise to take very good care of it."

"Thank *you*," said Henry. He brushed his hand across his eyes. "Well, I must say good-bye now. Enjoy the rest of your vacation."

Henry saluted them. Before Jack and Annie could say anything, the scientist turned and walked briskly back to the rowboat.

"Let's go," Annie said to Jack.

Jack and Annie walked around the dunes and headed through the sea grass to the rope ladder. Then they climbed back into the tree house and looked out the window. The rowboat was gliding over the shimmering water of the sunlit sea, heading back to the HMS *Challenger.*

"Good-bye, mates," said Jack.

"Our mission!" said Annie, as if she'd just remembered. She looked at Jack. "We didn't discover a secret of happiness!"

"Yes, we did," said Jack with a smile. "Henry said it, actually. A secret of happiness is having compassion for all living creatures."

"Compassion?" said Annie.

"Yeah, that means feeling sympathy and love for them," said Jack.

"Oh, sure," Annie said matter-of-factly. "Loving other creatures makes me really happy. I wonder why some people don't get that."

"I don't know," said Jack.

"Too bad they have to see a miracle first, like an octopus talking," said Annie.

"I know what you mean," said Jack. "The octopus just being an octopus is the real miracle."

Annie smiled. "And Henry's seashell—the little creature inside—him too," she said. "He was a miracle, too." She held out the shining shell.

Jack took the shell from her and carefully put it in his backpack. "The shell will help us remember the secret," he said.

"I think we always knew it," said Annie. "Henry just put it into words for us. Come on, let's go."

Annie picked up the Pennsylvania book and turned to the picture of the Frog Creek woods. "Lehhh meee gooo hooome," she said, repeating the strange sounds from the octopus.

Jack smiled. He started to tell her to say it right. But before he could, the tree house started to spin.

It spun faster and faster.

Then everything was still.

Absolutely still.

🐙 🐙 🐙

Soft raindrops pattered against the roof of the tree house.

"I love being home," said Annie.

"Me too," said Jack with a sigh.

Jack and Annie strapped on their bike helmets and pulled on their sneakers. Then Jack took their research book out of his pack and put in their library books.

"All I want to do now is go into our warm, dry house and see Mom and Dad," said Annie.

"Me too," said Jack. "And read one of my new library books."

"And eat dinner," said Annie.

"A *good* dinner," said Jack. "No stale biscuits or lime juice." He slipped on his backpack. "And *no* pea soup."

"Pea soup?" asked Annie.

But Jack had already started down the ladder. "And then read a little more and climb into bed," he continued.

"A warm, dry bed in a warm, dry house," said Annie, following him.

"Yep," said Jack, stepping onto the wet ground. "I guess the octopus just wanted to go home, too. Hey, I wonder if he has a name."

"Hmm . . . ," said Annie. She and Jack climbed on their bikes. "I think his name might be . . . *Charles!*"

"That sounds right," said Jack, laughing. "I wonder if Charles has an octopus wife—and octopus kids."

"I bet he does," said Annie. "And I bet he couldn't wait to get home and hold them in all eight of his arms."

Jack laughed again. "Yeah, I bet you're right," he said. Then he and Annie took off riding through the Frog Creek woods.

The rain fell harder. But it didn't matter. They were heading home.

Author's Notes

When I first decided to write about the deep sea, I had no idea where the story should take place or what sort of adventure should happen. Once I started my research, though, I discovered some exciting facts about ocean exploration in the 1800s. The ships that set sail were not seeking to discover new lands but rather to discover the depth, the life, and the structure of the world beneath the ocean. Many writers caught the romantic fever of writing about such voyages. The most famous of these stories was *20,000 Leagues Under the Sea* by Jules Verne.

The ship I decided to base my fictional story on was HMS *Challenger*, an English vessel that sailed nearly 70,000 miles between 1872 and 1876. During that time, the British scientists aboard the ship found more than 4,000 new living species of sea life! As well as gathering a huge number of plants and animals, their explorations gave the world a new understanding of the landscape of the deep sea, including how deep it is and that it has mountains and ridges just like the land above water.

When shell collecting was very popular in the 1800s, the most sought-after shell was the chambered nautilus. I learned in my research that during the actual voyage of HMS *Challenger*, a living chambered nautilus was captured in the South Pacific. When it was placed in a tub, the creature inside the shell swam around, ejecting water out of its funnel. I imagined this was the creature that Henry had so loved.

The character of Henry was inspired by a real

scientist who sailed aboard the *Challenger* named Henry Moseley. He was a young man in his twenties when the voyage began. He loved natural history and became one of the greatest natural scientists of his time. The chief scientist on the *Challenger* was Charles Wyville Thomson, a brilliant Scottish professor.

All the scientists aboard the ship were courageous explorers who gave birth to a new area of study called oceanography, which is a branch of knowledge concerning the earth's oceans and seas. Today oceanographers all over the world study climate change, global warming, water pollution, and related concerns. They are working hard to protect the precious life under the sea.

Turn the page for great activities!

Fun Activities for Jack and Annie and *You*!

Crafty Day in the Deep Sea!

Sea stars (also known as starfish) and other objects from the ocean can make beautiful decorations. But you don't need to comb the beach to get a sea star. You can make your own decoration that looks and feels just like the real thing!

Sea Star Decoration

You will need:

- Waxed paper
- Glue
- A paper clip
- Sand, cornmeal, and/or glitter
- String or yarn

1. On a piece of waxed paper, squeeze glue in the shape of a sea star. Carefully fill the whole shape in with glue. You should have a sea star–shaped blob of glue.

2. Bend a paper clip into an upside-down U shape. Stick the ends of the clip into the glue at the end of one arm of the star. This should form a little loop that will stick out from the end of the arm.

3. Lightly sprinkle sand, cornmeal, glitter, or any combination of the three over the glue. Try to cover the glue completely.

4. Shake the excess sand, cornmeal, and/or glitter off gently.

5. Leave out overnight to dry.

6. When the sea star is completely dry, carefully peel it away from the waxed paper.

7. Put a piece of string or yarn through the paper-clip loop to make a necklace or decoration that you can hang anywhere you like.

Enjoy!

Puzzle of the Deep Sea

Jack and Annie learned many new things on their deep-sea adventure. Did you?

Put your knowledge to the test with this puzzle. You can use a notebook or make a copy of this page if you don't want to write in your book.

1. The name of the ship that sailed in the 1870s to research the deep sea.

2. A small sea creature with a round spiral shell that swims by taking in water and shooting it back out.

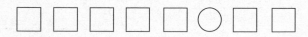

3. What the huge sea creature that the crew calls a sea monster really is.

☐ ☐ ☐ ☐ ☐

☐ ◯ ☐ ☐ ☐ ☐ ☐

4. The place on board the ship where the scientists and officers eat.

☐ ◯ ☐ ☐ ☐ ☐ ☐ ☐

5. The last name of the chief scientist on board the research ship.

☐ ☐ ☐ ☐ ◯ ☐ ☐

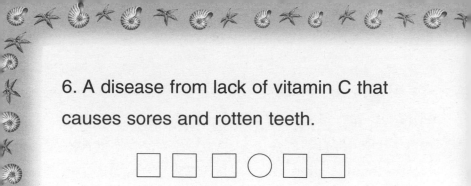

6. A disease from lack of vitamin C that causes sores and rotten teeth.

7. The scientific term for mud covering the ocean bottom.

□ □ □ ○

Now look at your answers above. The letters that are circled spell a word—but that word is scrambled! Can you unscramble it to spell the name Jack and Annie gave the creature who saved them?

Sal Murdocca is best known for his amazing work on the Magic Tree House series. He has written and/or illustrated over two hundred children's books, including *Dancing Granny* by Elizabeth Winthrop, *Double Trouble in Walla Walla* by Andrew Clements, and *Big Numbers* by Edward Packard. He has taught writing and illustration at the Parsons School of Design in New York. He is the librettist for a children's opera and has recently completed his second short film. Sal Murdocca is an avid runner, hiker, and bicyclist. He has often bicycle-toured in Europe and has had many one-man shows of his paintings from these trips. He lives and works with his wife, Nancy, in New City, New York.

MAGIC TREE HOUSE® BOOKS

<table>
<tr><td>#1: Dinosaurs Before Dark</td><td>#15: Viking Ships at Sunrise</td></tr>
<tr><td>#2: The Knight at Dawn</td><td>#16: Hour of the Olympics</td></tr>
<tr><td>#3: Mummies in the Morning</td><td>#17: Tonight on the Titanic</td></tr>
<tr><td>#4: Pirates Past Noon</td><td>#18: Buffalo Before Breakfast</td></tr>
<tr><td>#5: Night of the Ninjas</td><td>#19: Tigers at Twilight</td></tr>
<tr><td>#6: Afternoon on the Amazon</td><td>#20: Dingoes at Dinnertime</td></tr>
<tr><td>#7: Sunset of the Sabertooth</td><td>#21: Civil War on Sunday</td></tr>
<tr><td>#8: Midnight on the Moon</td><td>#22: Revolutionary War on Wednesday</td></tr>
<tr><td>#9: Dolphins at Daybreak</td><td>#23: Twister on Tuesday</td></tr>
<tr><td>#10: Ghost Town at Sundown</td><td>#24: Earthquake in the Early Morning</td></tr>
<tr><td>#11: Lions at Lunchtime</td><td>#25: Stage Fright on a Summer Night</td></tr>
<tr><td>#12: Polar Bears Past Bedtime</td><td>#26: Good Morning, Gorillas</td></tr>
<tr><td>#13: Vacation Under the Volcano</td><td>#27: Thanksgiving on Thursday</td></tr>
<tr><td>#14: Day of the Dragon King</td><td>#28: High Tide in Hawaii</td></tr>
</table>

...and continuing this series with

MERLIN MISSIONS

New!

Ask an adult to help you!

1. Cut out tattoo.

2. Peel off protective layer from tattoo.

3. Put tattoo facedown against skin, press firmly.

4. Wet back of tattoo with damp cloth or sponge.

5. Wait 30 seconds, slide paper backing off, and wipe lightly with wet cloth or sponge.

To remove, wipe gently with alcohol or baby oil.

NOTE: Do not apply to sensitive skin or near eyes.

Safe and nontoxic

Ingredients: Acrylate/VA Copolymer, Castor Oil, Ethyl Cellulose, Refined Shellac, Hydroxypropyl Cellulose, Titanium Dioxide, Carbon Black Pigment, FD&C Yellow #5 Aluminum Lake, FD&C Blue #1 Aluminum Lake, FD&C Red #7 (Calcium) Lake.

Tattoos manufactured in the U.S.A.
Illustrations © 2009 by Sal Murdocca

T-TT5-20598-0